W9-CFM-571

Gift For

_____

From

_____

Copyright © 2009 Hallmark Licensing, Inc.

Published by Hallmark Books,
a division of Hallmark Cards, Inc.,
Kansas City, MO 64141
Visit us on the Web at www.Hallmark.com.

All rights reserved. No part of this publication may be
reproduced, transmitted, or stored in any form or by any means
without the prior written permission of the publisher.

Editor: Michael Brush
Art Director: Michael Lee
Cover Designer: Michael Scheible

ISBN: 978-1-59530-217-5

XLJ6022

Printed and bound in China

The Story of
Santa's
Magic Pen

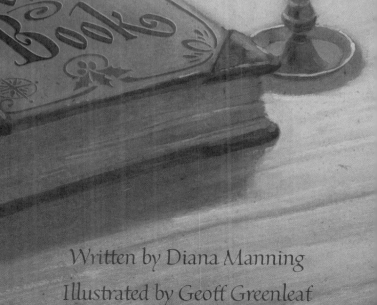

Written by Diana Manning

Illustrated by Geoff Greenleaf

It was early December,

and Santa's workshop was all in a jumble.

Santa had misplaced one of the lists he was always making,

and the elves were searching high and low.

All of the girls and boys on that list

would be awfully disappointed if it didn't turn up!

After locating the missing list under a pile of toys, Elmer, Santa's
trusted Elf-in-Charge, set to work on an early Christmas gift
to help Santa get organized. When Elmer was finished,
he assembled the other elves to help him
present his creation to Santa.

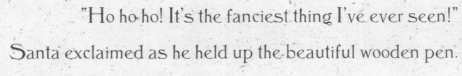

"Ho ho ho! It's the fanciest thing I've ever seen!"

Santa exclaimed as he held up the beautiful wooden pen.

"Why, that looks like my workshop on top . . .

and there's my reindeer . . .

and there's ME!"

"It's also magic," said Elmer. "Just try it out, Santa, and see what happens!"

So Santa took some paper and began making one of his famous lists.
Elmer held up Santa's Official North Pole Record Book,
where the list instantly appeared
as Santa wrote. All the elves
gasped in amazement.

"Jumpin' Jingle Bells, that's remarkable! How in the world does it work?" asked Santa.

"The magic's in the wood. It's carved from a branch of the North Pole Christmas Tree," Elmer answered. "Whenever you write something with this pen, it automatically appears in your Official Record Book. No more lost lists!"

"Hooray!" cheered the elves. Santa shook Elmer's hand and thanked him

for his clever thinking and beautiful handiwork.

Santa put the pen in his pocket

and carried it wherever he went,

just in case he needed

to jot something down.

But that was only the beginning. That very Christmas Eve, something happened that would make North Pole history. On one of his deliveries, as Santa bent down to arrange the gifts under the tree, his magic pen slipped out of his pocket and landed among the brightly wrapped packages.

The next morning, Santa's pen was discovered under the tree by a little girl named Merribelle. Now no one loved Christmas more than Merribelle. Even her name sounded like Christmas! And she was thrilled with what she thought was Santa's gift meant especially for her.

Back at the North Pole, Santa turned his pockets inside out and looked everywhere for his magic pen. As the days turned to months and there was no sign of the missing magic pen, Santa kept hoping that Elmer hadn't noticed.

It wasn't until a few weeks before the next Christmas that Santa's mistake finally came to light—and in the most curious way. As Santa and his elves were looking through his Official Record Book one day (and checking it twice), a letter began to show up on one of its pages . . .

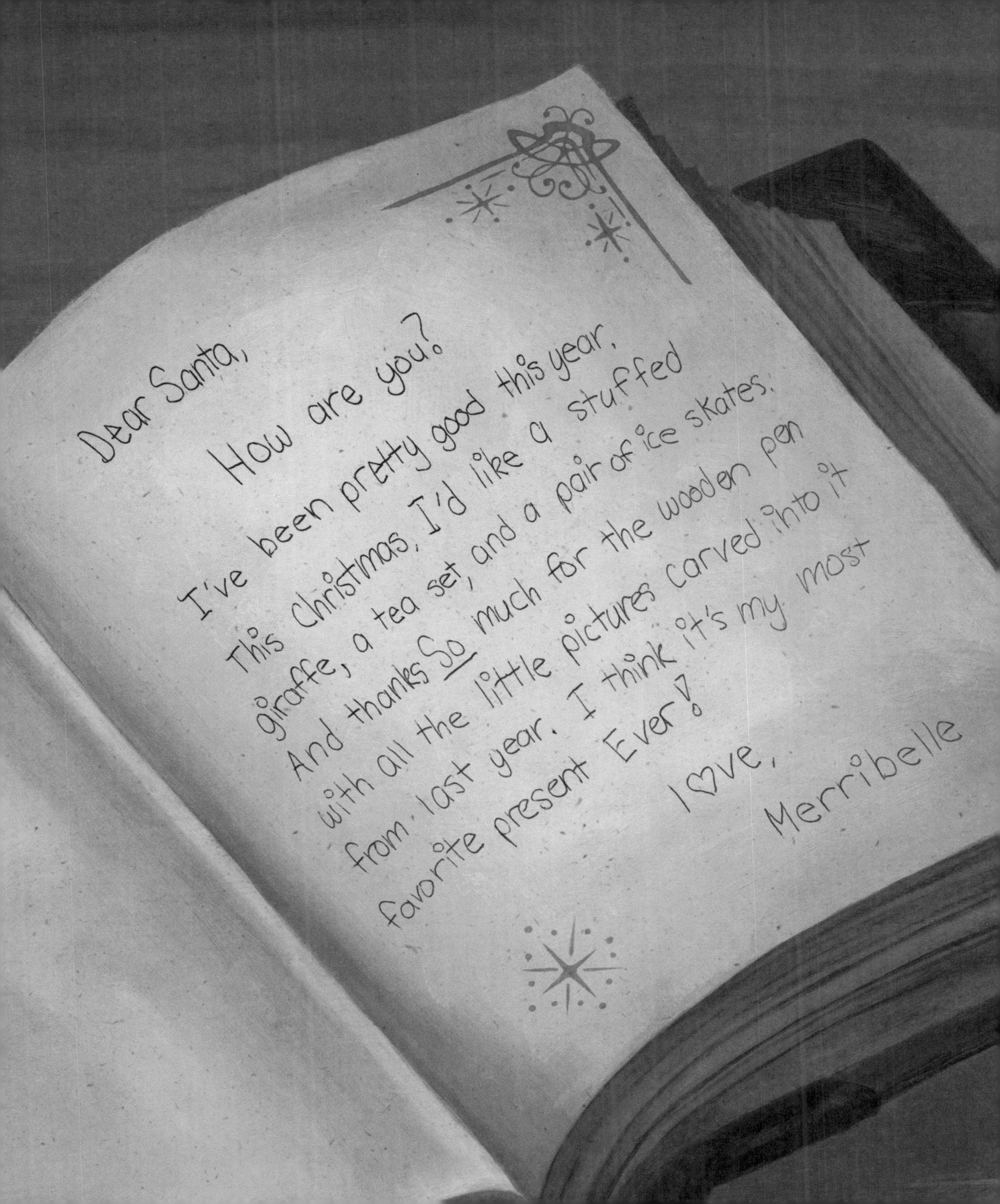

Dear Santa,

How are you?

I've been pretty good this year.

This Christmas, I'd like a stuffed giraffe, a tea set, and a pair of ice skates.

And thanks _So_ much for the wooden pen with all the little pictures carved into it from last year. I think it's my most favorite present Ever!

I♡ve,

Merribelle

"So **THAT'S** where the pen went," Elmer said as he started to laugh. "I was wondering what had happened to it!"

Santa's face turned as red as his suit. "Oh, ho, ho! I must have left it at Merribelle's house," he admitted sheepishly.

"It's all right, Santa. I can carve you another pen," Elmer assured him.

So Santa set about writing back to Merribelle about the pen and its special magic. He told her how her letter had appeared in his Official Record Book and how the magic came from the North Pole Christmas tree.

Before long, letters came pouring in asking for a magic pen "just like Merribelle's."

"You know, Santa, making pens for ALL the children isn't a bad idea," Elmer suggested. "If every child were to write to you with the magic pen, their letters would automatically show up in your Official Record Book."

"Rollicking Reindeer!" Santa exclaimed. "What a wonderful idea!
Why, this will forever change the way we do things around here.
We're going to get organized, I tell you!"

So Elmer quickly rallied the elves in a flurry of sawing
and sanding and carving. Soon Santa's magic
pens found their way into the hands
of children all around the world.

And that's the way it happened.

Elmer's clever idea to keep Santa organized

had done just that, and children everywhere

discovered a magical new way to write to Santa.

And though, of course, the children knew

he couldn't always promise everything on their lists,

just having the magic pen meant

knowing their letters would instantly appear

in Santa's Official Record Book . . .

right where they belonged!

Santa's waiting to hear from you!

Use your magic pen to write your

Christmas letter on the following pages!

To Santa

To Santa

To Santa

_____

_____

_____

_____

_____

_____

_____

_____

_____

_____

_____

To Santa

To Santa

To Santa

To Santa

To Santa

To Santa

To Santa

To Santa

If you had lots of fun with Santa's Magic Pen,

Hallmark would love to hear from you.

Send us a letter or an e-mail!

Book Feedback
Hallmark Cards, Inc.
2501 McGee Street
Mail Drop 215
Kansas City, MO 64108

booknotes@hallmark.com

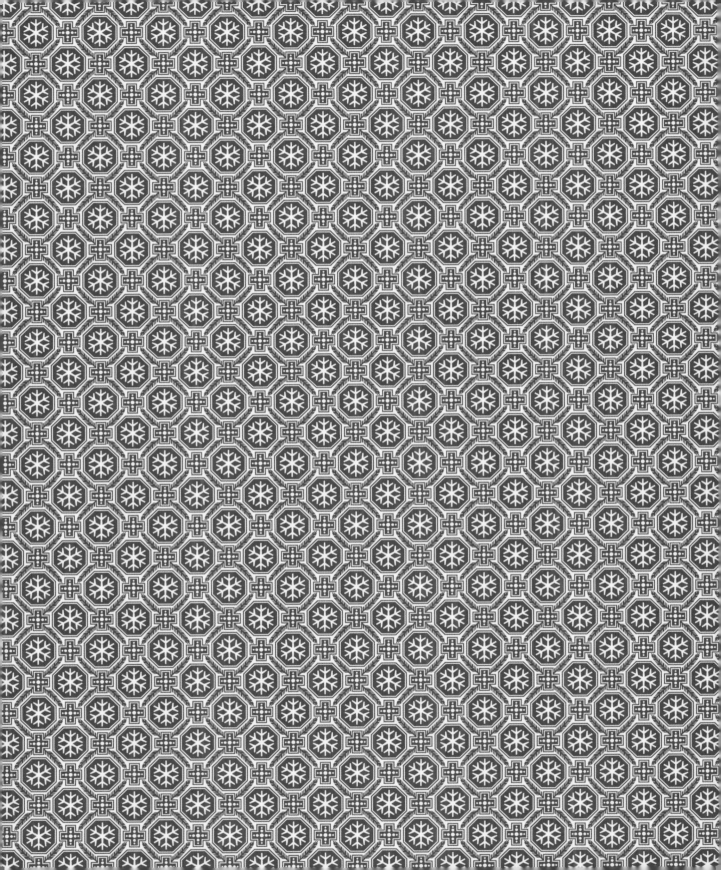